PANCHO RABBIT AND THE COYOTE

● A Migrant's Tale ●

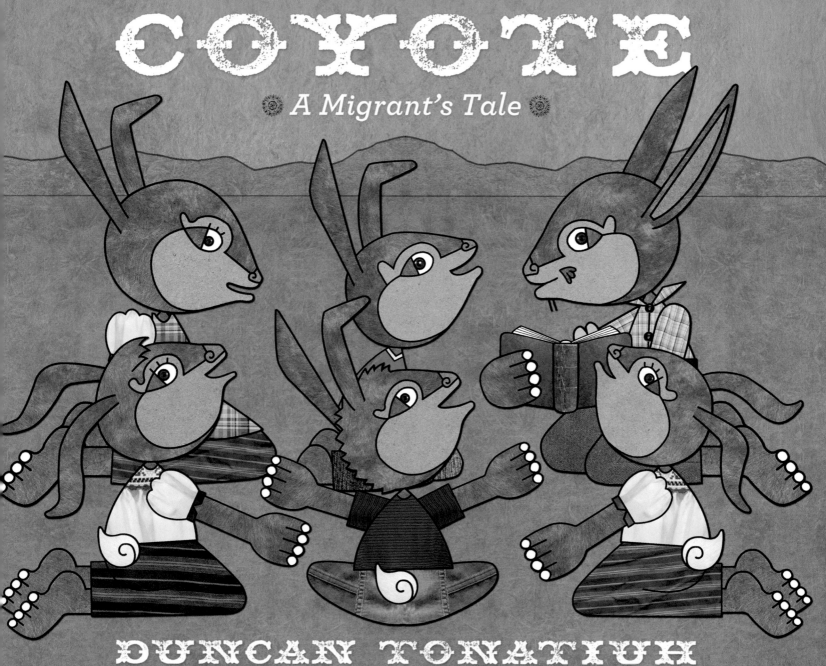

DUNCAN TONATIUH

Abrams Books for Young Readers ● New York

One spring the rains did not come and the crops could not grow. So Papá Rabbit, Señor Rooster, Señor Ram, and other animals from the *rancho* set out north to find work in the great carrot and lettuce fields. There they could earn money for their families.

Many harvests went by, and it was finally time for Papá Rabbit to return home. His family was preparing a big *fiesta*. Everyone on the rancho was excited to see him, especially Pancho Rabbit, his eldest son.

"I heard Mamá telling Señora Duck that Papá saved enough money in El Norte so that he won't ever have to leave us again," Pancho told his brother and sisters. They were helping Mamá cook Papá his favorite meal: *mole*, rice and beans, a heap of warm *tortillas*, and a jugful of fresh *aguamiel*.

The musicians arrived and began to tune their instruments while Pancho and his sister hung *papel picado* to decorate the patio. The Rabbits' friends from the rancho began to arrive.

They listened to the *música*. They ate some mole. And they waited and waited, but Papá Rabbit did not appear.

"He must have had a late start," said Mamá Rabbit.

"Maybe the weather was bad and he had to find shelter," said Pancho's youngest sister.

They waited some more, but still Papá Rabbit was not to be seen. When it was dark, the musicians and the guests said their good-byes and headed home. "Your *papá* will certainly arrive by morning," Señora Duck told Pancho and his family.

After waiting and worrying long into the night, the Rabbit family finally went to bed. Except for Pancho. *I have to find my father*, he thought. He packed Papá's favorite meal: mole, rice and beans, a heap of still-warm tortillas, and a jugful of fresh aguamiel. He placed it in a *mochila* to carry on his back and headed out.

Pancho followed the stars north. After walking awhile, he met a coyote. "Good evening, little rabbit. Where are you going?"

"Good evening, Señor Coyote. I'm going north to meet my papá, who has been working in the carrot and lettuce fields," replied Pancho.

"It'll take you days and days to get there on this trail," replied the coyote. "I can show you a shortcut. That is, if you give me that sweet and spicy mole you have. I smelled it a mile away."

Pancho did not wish to give his father's mole away, but he missed him terribly. "As long as it gets me closer to Papá," he said, and he let the coyote have it.

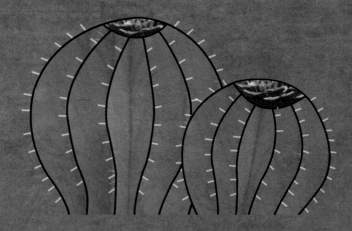

The coyote led Pancho to the train tracks. As the sun rose, he showed Pancho how to jump onto a passing car. The train was running so fast, poor Pancho almost fell off!

They rode atop the train, zooming through the countryside. When the train slowed for a curve, Pancho and the coyote leaped off.

"We must now cross this river," said the coyote.

"Señor Coyote, I don't know how to swim," said Pancho. The water was murky and rushed by very fast. He was scared.

"I can help you reach the other side," said the coyote, "but I will be exhausted after I do. Once we are across, I will need to eat the rice and beans you are carrying to regain my strength."

"Fine," said Pancho. "As long as it gets me closer to Papá."

The coyote picked up a tire that was junked on the riverbank. Pancho gathered all his courage and held on tight. *Splash!* They jumped into the river! The coyote helped him float to the far bank. And although he did not want to, Pancho gave the coyote the rice and beans, just as he'd promised.

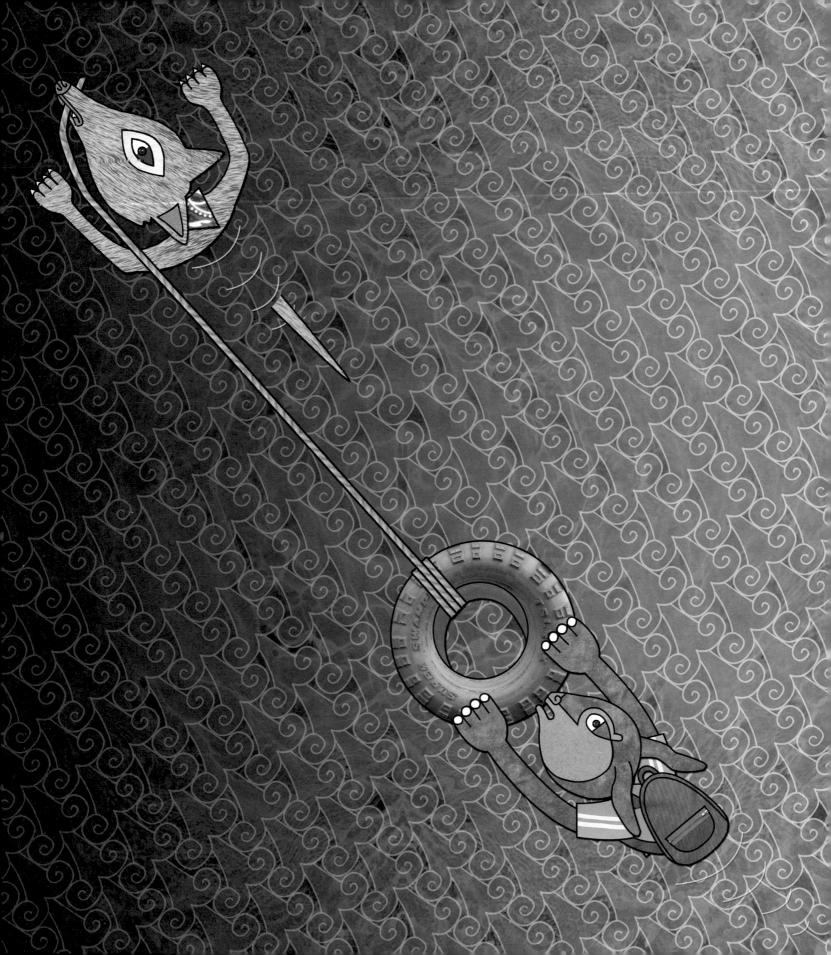

The sun was high in the sky now. Pancho and the coyote walked on and soon reached a very tall fence that separated the South from the North. It was impossible to jump or climb over. "There is a tunnel we can use," said the coyote, "but the snakes watch it. If you give them the tortillas you are carrying, I'm sure they will let us through."

"As long as it gets me closer to Papá," Pancho said and sighed.

The coyote talked to the snakes. They agreed to let them pass but demanded every single one of Pancho's tortillas. Pancho and the coyote entered the tunnel. It was dark, narrow, and very long.

When they emerged, Pancho and the coyote were on the north side of the fence. They were in El Norte! The afternoon sun beat down on them, and there was no shade. The coyote pointed to a hut in the distance. "We can spend the night there," he said. "In the morning I will take you to the great carrot and lettuce fields, and there you will find your papá."

Pancho and the coyote walked under the desert sun. Poor Pancho's feet ached. "Give me some of that aguamiel you have, little rabbit," said the coyote. "I feel dizzy. If I don't drink something, I will collapse and we will never get there."

Pancho gave the coyote some aguamiel. The sand and air were scorching hot, and Pancho felt dizzy. He was very thirsty, and he drank the remainder. "As long as it gets me closer to Papá," repeated Pancho to himself in a daze.

When Pancho and the coyote reached the hut, it was dark. The
coyote built a small fire for light and warmth, because at night the
desert is freezing cold. "I am so hungry after all that walking," said the
coyote. "Do you have any more mole, little rabbit?"

"No, Señor Coyote. You ate it all."

"Any more rice and beans?"

"No, Señor Coyote. You ate them all."

"Any more tortillas?"

"No, Señor Coyote. The snakes ate them all. There is nothing left, not
even a drop of aguamiel."

"In that case," said the coyote, "I will roast you in the fire and eat
you!"

With a cry Pancho leapt for the door. He was the fastest animal back on the rancho, and normally he could outrun the coyote. But he was tired from the long journey. He could not reach the door. He could not reach the window. All he could do was huddle in a corner as the coyote slowly approached.

Suddenly the door was thrown open. Who entered but Papá Rabbit, with Señor Ram and Señor Rooster! They soon had the coyote racing outdoors and far away with his tail between his legs.

"*Panchito! Mijó!*" said Papá Rabbit, and he gave Pancho a hug. "I thought I would never see you again!"

"A gang of crows attacked us," said Señor Rooster. "They took the money and gifts we were bringing back to our families and left us stranded in the desert."

"We heard your cries for help," said Señor Ram. "Your papá recognized your voice. We ran to you as fast as we could."

"Papá!" said Pancho. "I am so happy to find you. And I know the way home!"

So Pancho led Papá Rabbit, Señor Rooster, and Señor Ram home. When they arrived, there was a big fiesta. There was mole, rice and beans, warm tortillas, fresh aguamiel, and música for everyone on the rancho.

Pancho told his brother and sisters about all the dangers he and Papá had faced. "Please don't leave us again," said the Rabbit children. "We were so worried for you."

"I don't want to leave you," said Papá Rabbit, "but the crows took all our money. If it doesn't rain enough again this year, and if there is no food or work here on the rancho, what else am I to do? I will have to leave again."

"And I will come with you," said Pancho.

"We will all go with you," said Pancho's brother and sisters.

"Let's hope it rains," said Mamá.

●AUTHOR'S NOTE●

In Spanish the word coyote has two meanings. It is the name of an animal, but it is also slang for a person who smuggles people between the U.S. and Mexican border.

I am fortunate in many ways. I was raised in a middle class family in Mexico. My mother is Mexican and my father is American. I have dual citizenship and I can enter and leave the U.S. and Mexico whenever I choose. I was able to attend high school and college in America. Most of the kids in my *colonia*, or neighborhood, in San Miguel de Allende are not so fortunate. They did not expect to go to college or pursue careers. Their highest expectation was to become *albañiles*, to carry bricks and mix cement as part of the workforce. Many left for the U.S. by the time they turned eighteen years old.

When they came back to San Miguel (either on their own or having been deported), they told stories about eating snake when they ran out of food while crossing the desert, or of waiting for days in a shanty house in a border town for the coyote to show up. One of my neighbors—we used to play hockey with sticks and limes from a tree—died of dehydration while trying to cross.

According to a 2010 Pew Research Center report, 11.2 million undocumented immigrants live in the U.S. Most of them are from Mexico, Central America, and the Caribbean. An average of 150,000 unauthorized immigrants enter the U.S. each year. The number was triple that in the early 2000s before the economic recession.

According to Amnesty International, immigrants leave their home countries mostly due to poverty and lack of opportunities at home. They come to the U.S. looking for work and for a better life for themselves and their families. Immigrants pay coyotes exorbitant fees and risk their lives to reach their destination. They encounter terrible dangers throughout their journey. Central American immigrants travel around five thousand miles on top of trains to cross Mexico. They are often victims of gang violence because they lack protection from the authorities due to their unauthorized status.

Some migrants never reach their destination. According to the American Civil Liberties Union and Mexico's National Human Rights Commission (Comisión Nacional de los Derechos Humanos, CNDH), between 350 and 500 migrants die every year from violence, drowning, or dehydration while crossing the desert to reach the U.S.

Illegal immigration is a complicated issue that involves the U.S., Mexican, and Central American governments and societies. On the one hand the immigrants' home countries have to improve living conditions and create better opportunities for their citizens so that they are not forced to look to the outside for answers. On the other hand the U.S. needs to admit its dependency on undocumented workers to do much of its manual and domestic labor and to provide legal and safe working opportunities for those seeking employment. Undocumented immigrants are a huge and important part of the U.S. workforce. According to a Pew Research Center study in 2005, 7.2 million undocumented workers were working in low skilled and often grueling jobs, like farming and construction. Only 31% of U.S.-born workers hold those occupations.

Undocumented workers earn less than their American counterparts. More than half of adult unauthorized immigrants (59%) had no health insurance during all of 2007. Because of their unauthorized status, they are forced to live in the shadows and they are scared to seek protection against unfair and unscrupulous employers.

There have been developments in immigration reform in recent years, both pro and anti-immigrant. The harsh legislation of SB 1070 in Arizona, for instance, targets immigrants. There is also legislation like the DREAM Act being discussed, which will offer a way for undocumented immigrants that came to the U.S. as children to become lawful permanent residents after they complete a number of years in military service or higher education. Yet, no comprehensive reform that gets at the root of the issue has been created.

We often hear of immigrants in the media, however too often with negative and sensational tones. Undocumented immigrants are often equated with terrorists and drug traffickers, when in reality almost all immigrants are hard working people trying to provide for their families. In 2008, 94% of undocumented immigrant men of working age were employed, compared to 83% of U.S.-born men.

We seldom see the dangerous journey immigrants go through to reach the U.S. and the longing that their families feel for them back at home. It is my desire that *Pancho Rabbit and the Coyote: A Migrant's Tale* captures some of that sentiment; ironically, the animals convey the *human* emotions and side of the story. I hope this book will help teachers, librarians, and parents spark conversations with young people about this critical issue.

Further, there are an estimated 1.5 million undocumented children in the U.S., and according to a 2011 Pew Hispanic Center report, in 2008 there were 5.5 million children of illegal immigrants in U.S. schools. I think that a lot of those children will relate to *Pancho Rabbit*.

References and websites where you can read more:

- http://pewresearch.org/topics/immigration/
- http://pewresearch.org/pubs/1876/unauthorized-immigrant-population-united-states-national-state-trends-2010
- http://pewresearch.org/pubs/1190/portrait-unauthorized-immigrants-states
- http://www.pewhispanic.org/2006/03/07/size-and-characteristics-of-the-unauthorized-migrant-population-in-the-us/
- http://www.washingtonpost.com/wp-dyn/content/article/2009/09/29/AR2009092903212.html
- http://www.amnesty.org/en/library/asset/AMR41/014/2010/en/8459f0ac-03ce-4302-8bd2-3305bdae9cde/amr410142010eng.pdf
- http://www.cndh.org.mx/Informes_Especiales

⊛ GLOSSARY ⊛

- *aguamiel*: a drink made from the sap of the maguey plant

- El Norte: literally "The North"; in Mexico, an informal way to refer to the United States

- *fiesta*: party

- *mamá*: mother

- *mijó*: a contraction of *mi hijo*, "my son." It is used as a term of endearment.

- *mochila*: backpack

- *mole*: a sweet and spicy sauce made with chiles, peanuts, and unsweetened chocolate among other ingredients

- *música*: music

- *Panchito*: little Pancho; an endearment

- *papá*: father

- *papel picado*: perforated paper. It is a decorative Mexican craft made from paper cut into elaborate designs. It is often hung from string and used prominently at parties and on holidays like *Día de los Muertos*, "the Day of the Dead."

- *rancho*: ranch

- señor: courtesy title similar to Mr. in English

- señora: courtesy title similar to Mrs. in English

- *tortilla*: a thin corn pancake-like disk

To Guadalupe, Yolanda (my mamá Duck), las patronas, and to the journey.

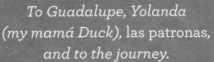
THE ARTWORK IN THIS BOOK IS HAND DRAWN, THEN COLLAGED DIGITALLY.

Library of Congress Cataloging-in-Publication Data
Tonatiuh, Duncan.
Pancho Rabbit and the coyote : a migrant's tale / by Duncan Tonatiuh.
p. cm.
Summary: When Papa Rabbit does not return home as expected from many seasons of working in the great carrot and lettuce fields of El Norte, his son Pancho sets out on a dangerous trek to find him, guided by a coyote. Includes author's note.
ISBN 978-1-4197-0583-0
[1. Voyages and travels—Fiction. 2. Migrant labor—Fiction. 3. Rabbits—Fiction. 4. Coyote—Fiction. 5. Allegories.] I. Title.
PZ7.T66414Pan 2013
[E] —dc23
2012022573

Text and illustrations copyright © 2013 Duncan Tonatiuh
Book design by Maria T. Middleton

Printed and bound in the USA
15 14 13 12 11 10 9 8 7

Abrams Books for Young Readers are available at special discounts when purchased in quantity for premiums and promotions as well as fundraising or educational use. Special editions can also be created to specification. For details, contact specialsales@abramsbooks.com or the address below.

ABRAMS The Art of Books
115 West 18th Street, New York, NY 10011
abramsbooks.com